Look What I Can Do

By Linda Hayward
Illustrated by Richard Brown

A SESAME STREET/GOLDEN PRESS BOOK
Published by Western Publishing Company, Inc.
in conjunction with Children's Television Workshop.

Look what I can do.
I can cut out pictures.

I can carry my plate to the kitchen sink.

Look what I can do.
I can hang up my towel.

I can build with blocks!

I can clean up a spill.

I can climb to the top.

Look what Cookie Monster can do.
He can measure the flour.
He can mix the dough.

I can paint a picture.

I can push the number four button.

I can fold my clothes.

I can feed my pet.

We can rake the leaves.
Just look what we can do.

AB